MOSHI monsters™

THE NIGHT BEFORE TWISTMAS

Published by Ladybird Books Ltd 2012
A Penguin Company
Penguin Books Ltd, 80 Strand, London, WC2R 0RL, UK
Penguin Group (USA) Inc., 375 Hudson Street, New York 10014, USA
Penguin Books Australia Ltd, Camberwell Road, Camberwell, Victoria 3124,
Australia (A division of Pearson Australia Group Pty Ltd)
Canada, India, New Zealand, South Africa

Written by Jonathan Green (After Clement Clarke Moore)
Illustrations by Vincent Bechet, Lea Wade and Trevor White
Sunbird is a trademark of Ladybird Books Ltd

www.ladybird.com

ISBN: 978-1-40939-140-1
10 9 8 7 6 5 4 3 2 1
Printed in Slovakia

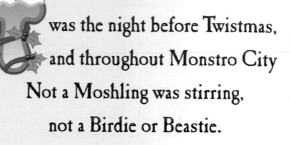'T was the night before Twistmas,
and throughout Monstro City
Not a Moshling was stirring,
not a Birdie or Beastie.

arge signs had been placed
to be seen from the sky,
In hopes that a bearer of gifts
would drop by.

he Moshis were sleeping,
tucked up in their beds,
While visions of barfmallows
danced in their heads.
And down on his ranch
Buster Bumblechops snored,
Dreaming of Moshlings
and lands unexplored.

hen out in Main Street —
not a phantom, but real —
There arrived the most
terrible automobile.
And out of the car climbed a sinister figure,
In his hand was a cane;
at its end was a trigger.

neaky and sly and just
ever so shifty,
He wore a top hat and his
coat looked quite nifty.
The buttons were gold like the tip of his cane,
And if you'd been there you'd have
heard this refrain:

'm Strangeglove, I'm Strangeglove.
They call me Dr. Strangeglove!
Musky Huskies must beware,
I'm no fan of puppy love!"

hen from their hidey-holes,

his servants they came,

And when Strangeglove called them,

he called them by name.

19

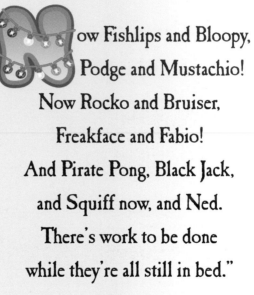

"**N**ow Fishlips and Bloopy,

Podge and Mustachio!

Now Rocko and Bruiser,

Freakface and Fabio!

And Pirate Pong, Black Jack,

and Squiff now, and Ned.

There's work to be done

while they're all still in bed."

21

he time, Glumps, has come,

for my plan's activation.

Take it all down,

every last decoration!

Those stupid trees too,

every signpost must go.

Twistmas is cancelled!

And get rid of the snow."

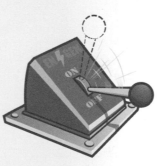

ith the monsters still sleeping,
the Glumps set to work,
Dr. Strangeglove directing,
with a sneer and a smirk.
They took down the tinsel,
then just out of spite,
They broke into En-Gen,
and turned out the lights.

24

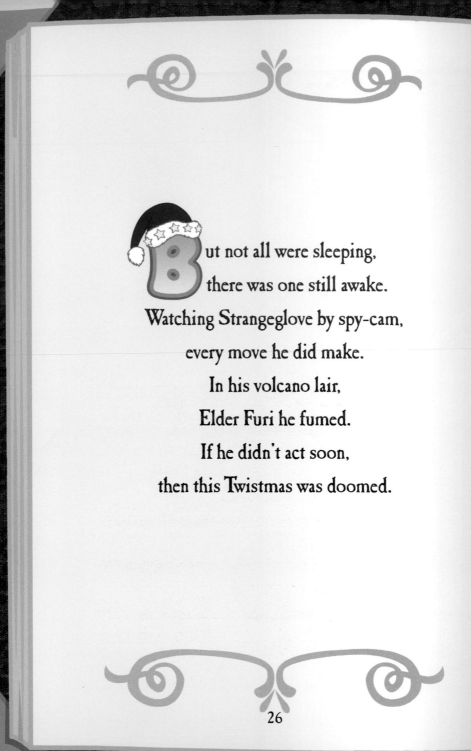

But not all were sleeping,
there was one still awake.
Watching Strangeglove by spy-cam,
every move he did make.
In his volcano lair,
Elder Furi he fumed.
If he didn't act soon,
then this Twistmas was doomed.

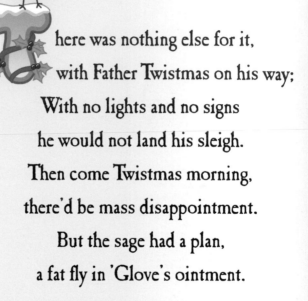

here was nothing else for it,

with Father Twistmas on his way;

With no lights and no signs

he would not land his sleigh.

Then come Twistmas morning,

there'd be mass disappointment.

But the sage had a plan,

a fat fly in 'Glove's ointment.

ow the sage and the scoundrel
had once been good friends,
'Til the doc used his gifts
for more criminal ends.
Furi'd stop Strangeglove yet,
that old party pooper,
So he put out the call,
for the Moshis called Super.

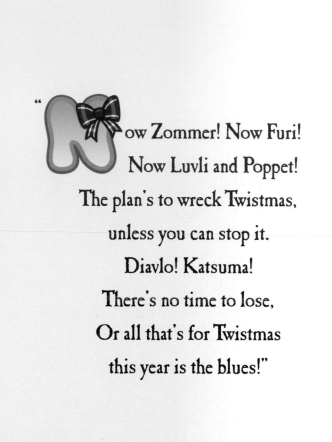

"Now Zommer! Now Furi!
Now Luvli and Poppet!
The plan's to wreck Twistmas,
unless you can stop it.
Diavlo! Katsuma!
There's no time to lose,
Or all that's for Twistmas
this year is the blues!"

And then, in a twinkling,
of old Furi's eye
The Supers came hurtling
out of the sky.

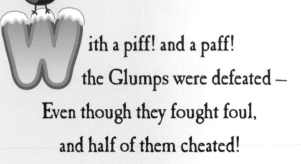

With a piff! and a paff!
the Glumps were defeated –
Even though they fought foul,
and half of them cheated!

37

"t's almost past midnight,"
Dr. Strangeglove declared,
"And the lights are still off
and the signs unprepared,
Which means Father Twistmas is going
to miss Monstro City!
Despite all you've done,
I've still won! What a pity."

earing the jingle
of sleigh-bells above,
They scowled at the rogue,
mad Dr. Strangeglove,
While high in the heavens,
a sled crossed the sky.
They'd run out of time –
that they couldn't deny.

uri was furious,
Poppet was pouting,
Katsuma went crazy,
and Zommer was shouting.
Only Luvli said nothing,
her eyes on Diavlo,
For the hot-headed Moshi
was feeling quite aggro.

43

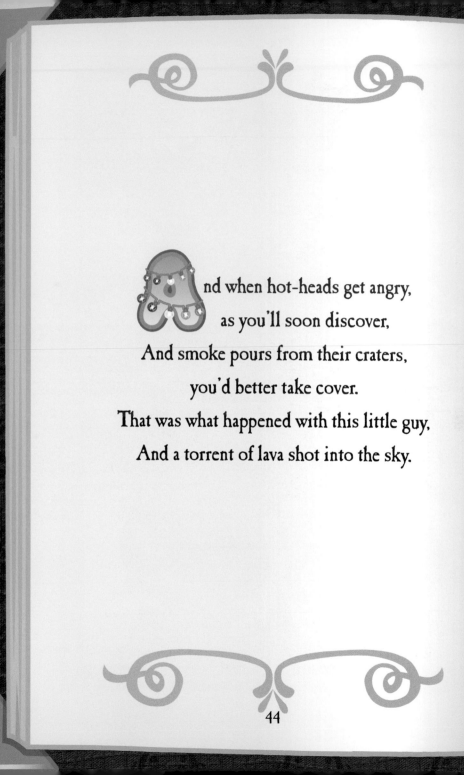

nd when hot-heads get angry,

as you'll soon discover,

And smoke pours from their craters,

you'd better take cover.

That was what happened with this little guy,

And a torrent of lava shot into the sky.

hey all heard the screech
of brakes high overhead,
Then the jingling resumed,
and down the sled sped.
It came in to land
by the Gross-ery Store,
Following the glow
to Snozz Wobbleson's door.

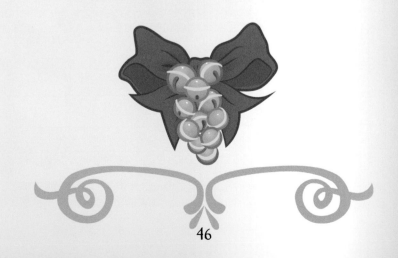

ather Twistmas gave a laugh,
and then gave a chuckle,
Put the sleigh into park
and unfastened the buckle,
Then letting his seatbelt
fly back into place,
He greeted them all
with a smile on his face.

ather Twistmas stepped down
from the driver's position,
The Moshis felt proud;
they'd completed their mission.
Their stockings would be filled,
right up to the brim,
But for 'Glove and his Glumps,
the future looked grim.

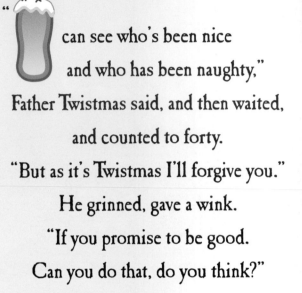

can see who's been nice

and who has been naughty,"

Father Twistmas said, and then waited,

and counted to forty.

"But as it's Twistmas I'll forgive you."

He grinned, gave a wink.

"If you promise to be good.

Can you do that, do you think?"

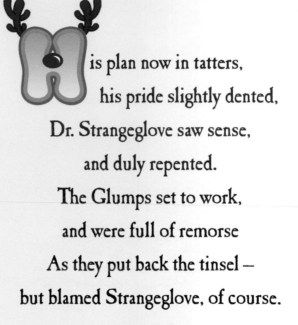

is plan now in tatters,

his pride slightly dented,

Dr. Strangeglove saw sense,

and duly repented.

The Glumps set to work,

and were full of remorse

As they put back the tinsel –

but blamed Strangeglove, of course.

s TickTocks chimed midnight,
all over the town,
From out of their houses,
the monsters came down
To meet Father Twistmas,
their presents to get –
And all agreed
it was the best Twistmas yet.

is sack of toys empty,

    Father Twistmas started his sleigh —

The reindeer leapt skyward,

    and then were away.

But his voice echoed after,

    as he flew out of sight,

Happy Twistmas to all . . .

and to all a good night!"

THE END